# Sammy the Elephant & Mr Camel

To all the natural abilities
within all children
*Joyce and Richard*

To Freddie R.
*Germaine*

# Sammy the Elephant & Mr Camel

Joyce C Mills, PhD &
Richard J Crowley, PhD

illustrated by
Germaine Cook

A Story to Help Children Overcome Bedwetting
While Discovering Self-Appreciation

**Magination Press**
**A Division of Brunner/Mazel, Inc.**
**New York**

**Library of Congress Cataloging-in-Publication Data**

Mills, Joyce C., 1944–
    Sammy the elephant and Mr. Camel

    Summary: With Mr. Camel's help, Sammy the Elephant
learns to strengthen his trunk muscles so he is finally able
to assume his circus duty of carrying water and appreciate
all the other things he can do too.
    [1. Self-realization—Fiction.   2. Elephants—
Fiction.   3. Camels—Fiction]   I. Crowley, Richard J.,
1942–    .   II. Cook, Germaine, ill.   III. Title.
PZ7.M63977Sam   1988         [E]         88-13581
ISBN 0-945354-09-6
ISBN 0-945354-08-8 (pbk.)

*Published by*
**Magination Press**
An Imprint of Brunner/Mazel, Inc., 19 Union Square West, New York, NY 10003

*Paperback edition distributed to the trade by*
**Publishers Group West**
4065 Hollis St., Emoryville, CA 94608
Telephone 800-982-8319; in CA call collect 415-658-3453

*Distributed in Canada by*
**Book Center**
1140 Beaulac St., Montreal, Quebec H4R 1R8, Canada

MANUFACTURED IN THE UNITED STATES OF AMERICA

10 9 8 7 6 5 4 3 2

# INTRODUCTION FOR PARENTS

*Sammy the Elephant and Mr. Camel* is a delightful and profound story that can be enjoyed by children of all ages. Although the story was originally created for a young boy who was a bedwetter, we have found that its theme of a struggling youngster who is guided to discover his own unique abilities can touch the heart of any child in a universal way.

When we presented *Sammy the Elephant and Mr. Camel* to our young client, we offered it simply as an enjoyable story. He was never told that the story had anything to do with his bedwetting problem. On a conscious level, the little boy delighted in the story line of Sammy, a lovable little elephant who kept spilling his buckets of water. At the same time, on an unconscious level, he was being given a comprehensive healing metaphor — a symbolic story — which mirrored his own failure and frustrations in attempting to gain control over his bedwetting.

Other issues depicted by Sammy in the story include the problems of sadness and criticism that all children experience at one time or another, and the pain and isolation of feeling different.

As the story unfolds, Sammy the Elephant, together with our young listener, is re-introduced to his own inner strengths and abilities through the guidance of Mr. Camel. After Sammy goes through a learning period during which he has the pleasure of discovering how many things he can do well, there is a crisis — a fire near the circus — and a resolution, as Sammy saves the day. He has, indeed, learned many new things with the help of Mr. Camel. Sammy emerges from his experience with a new sense of self-appreciation. Children reading the story, or having it read to them, will also learn new ways to feel better about themselves, as they travel with Sammy and Mr. Camel.

You may read *Sammy the Elephant and Mr. Camel* to your child simply as an entertaining story. Or, if you choose, you may read it *slowly,* emphasizing the words in italics by making your voice softer or deeper. This subtle shift in your voice helps to activate your child's inner strengths and abilities in a special way.

The beauty of this kind of storytelling is that it enables children to apply the many learnings interwoven throughout the story to other areas of their lives where issues of control and self-appreciation are important.

Perhaps as you read this story to your child, you, too, may notice the many discoveries made available to you in delightful and surprising ways from your own *child within.*

This is the story of Sammy the Elephant and Mr. Camel. It takes place at a circus, which is being set up in the middle of a great field just outside of a small town.

Imagine the excitement, hearing the shouting and stomping, watching everyone doing their job, getting everything just where it needs to be in order to put up the big tent.

The tent is so big it *can easily hold everything within* it — all the people, the animals, the acrobats, the jugglers, the tightrope walkers, the trapeze artists, the clowns, the dancing bears, and even the lions who leap through flaming hoops.

As you already know, the animals help put the circus together. The animals are a very important part of the circus. Especially the elephants. The elephants carry the heavy buckets of water and the big heavy beams that hold up the tent. The elephants move the beams and the water buckets by carrying them in their trunks.

Imagine looking at a large elephant and watching him carry a heavy beam, hearing the sound the elephant makes, seeing how comfortably he carries the beam.

At the circus where this story happens, all of the elephants were doing their work very well. All except for one small elephant named Sammy.

Little Sammy went over, just like all the other elephants. He took his trunk and wrapped it around the handle of a large bucket of water. He began to lift it and to *hold it*, but very soon...BOOM!...it fell to the ground.

Imagine the sound as the bucket landed. Imagine seeing it begin to roll.

Sammy hoped that nobody had noticed what he had done. But the other animals started yelling, "What did you do that for?"

"It almost rolled over my paw!" roared Fritz the Lion.

"Can't you grab hold of it? Can't you *hold onto it longer,* the way everyone else does?" bellowed Harriet the Oldest Elephant.

Sammy got scared.

Sammy decided that maybe he hadn't paid enough attention. So he began to watch the other elephants carry the water and the heavy beams. He watched them very closely.

Then he went back and tried again. *Using all those muscles within* that trunk of his, Sammy wrapped it around the handle of the bucket. He picked up the bucket easily.

Sammy *felt really good inside* as he walked along, swaying from side to side, bringing it over to where they needed it.

But suddenly...BOOM!...down again! This time the bucket rolled so far that it knocked over all the other buckets. The water spilled everywhere.

Everyone was very angry with Sammy.

"Can't *you control that* bucket yet?" yelled Jeremiah the Giraffe.

*"You can hold that water,"* added Phillipa the Tiger. "All the elephants do. They *hold it very well.* Just watch what they do to carry the water in their trunks."

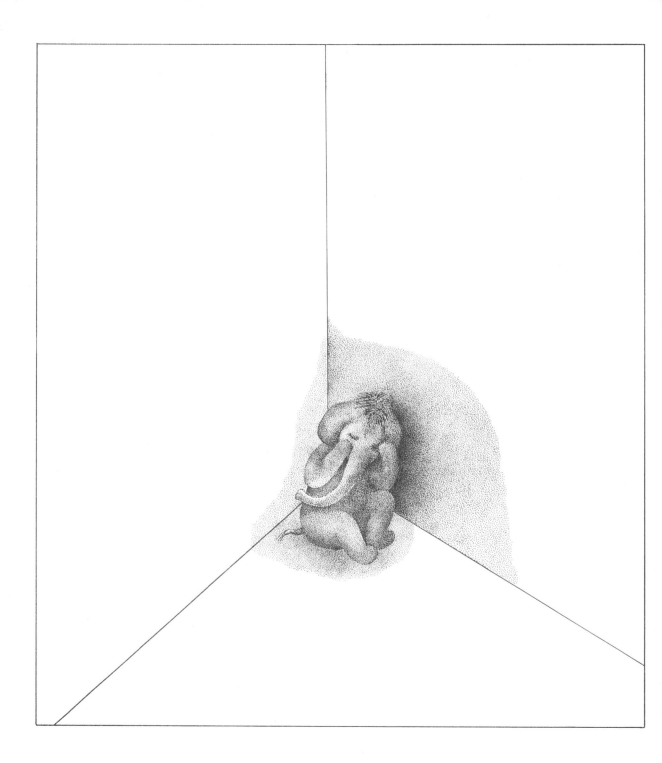

Well, by now Sammy was quite frustrated. Imagine how he felt. He tried and tried, day after day. But...BOOM!...down went the bucket of water every time he tried. He felt all the animals looking at him so meanly. He could tell that they were very upset with him. Sammy did not know what to do to please them. He felt ashamed of himself, and sad.

At times he would go off by himself and cry. "No one understands," he mumbled. "No one really cares."

One day when Sammy was feeling very sad, Mr. Camel heard him sniffling.

"You don't look very happy, Sammy," he said. "Is there anything I can do to help you feel better?"

"I don't know," Sammy answered. "I keep trying to *hold onto that* bucket, to do my part. But I keep spilling it. I keep letting it go too soon."

Mr. Camel thought for a moment. Then he began reminding Sammy of all the things that Sammy had learned to do since he had been in the circus.

"When you were born," said Mr. Camel, "you couldn't walk right away. There was a time when your legs were shaky. *You had to learn* to take each step, one after the other. At first you had a hard time, but *you continued to practice and to learn.* After a while, you learned to walk successfully."

"You also learned how to pick up grass with your trunk and eat it," Mr. Camel reminded Sammy. "*You learned* how to eat all by yourself. Now your trunk can carry just the right amount of food to satisfy you. *You learned to know when you are full and comfortable,* when you feel good inside. You may be surprised to realize how long *you can hold onto that good feeling. Now you can hold onto that good feeling for a long, long time,* Sammy."

Sammy thought for a few minutes and then answered, "Yes, I remember that. I can do that."

"It's just like Bonnie the Bicyclist," continued Mr. Camel. "I remember when she couldn't even ride a bicycle. She would get up on her bike, and fall down. As a matter of fact, someone had to teach Bonnie how to *hold on* to the handlebars correctly. She had to practice for a long time. After she *learned to hold on,* she was finally able to *relax and enjoy the feeling of letting go.*

"When you watch her, Sammy," Mr. Camel advised, "pay attention to that look on her face and notice the fun she is having *being in control* of her bicycle."

"Telling you about Bonnie," mused Mr. Camel, "reminds me of Jingles the Juggler. I remember when Jingles first came to the circus. All he could juggle were two little bowling pins.

"Now he can juggle balls, and large bowling pins, and dishes. He can juggle all those things together at the same time. His balance is perfect. He *knows exactly when to hold on and when to let go* of each of those items.

"You just have to *trust you can do it.* Some things take a little more time to learn than others, Sammy. And you have all the time in the world, all the time you need to *learn that now.*"

Suddenly Sammy and Mr. Camel heard sirens. They looked up and saw flames in the distance.

"It looks like there's a fire at that farmhouse way over there," Mr. Camel said. "But the fire engines won't be able to get there because the bridge is washed out. The only way to put out that fire is for the elephants to carry water in their trunks and spray it on the fire. But the other elephants are way across town practicing for the opening day parade."

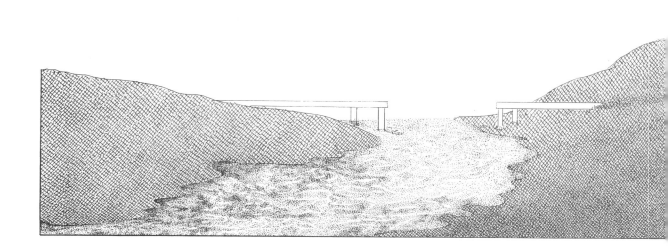

Little Sammy looked at Mr. Camel curiously. "Well, what
are we to do?" he asked.

"It's up to you now," Mr. Camel replied.

"What do you mean?" asked Sammy.

"I'm going to teach you something important," said Mr. Camel. "Listen very closely. As you know, camels *carry water for a long, long time.* I'm going to teach you how to do that, so *you can carry water for a long time,* too. And once *you can learn to do that,* you will be able to go over to the lake, put your trunk in, hear the water going into your trunk, and *hold onto it for a long time. You will be able to hold onto it successfully.*

"Then you will see yourself walking over to where the fire is and putting out the fire by *letting go of the water at just the right time and in just the right place.* Not a hundred feet before, not ten feet before, not even one foot before—but only when you are at exactly the right spot. Then you will aim your trunk and let go of all the water."

"Just remember a time when you held onto a special happy feeling for a long time," continued Mr. Camel. "Maybe you carried the excitement for a long time, wondering what gift you would be getting on your birthday. Everyone knows elephants have good memories and always remember everything that is important. *Remember something important you learned a long time ago and still carry happily with you now.*"

"After listening to you, Mr. Camel," said Sammy, "I can see myself doing all of that. I feel I can do it now."

So Mr. Camel and Sammy went over to the lake, and Sammy took in as much water as he could hold comfortably.

Then Sammy began the long walk over to the fire. Sammy got all the way to the fire.

Then, just as Mr. Camel had told him, Sammy let go of all the water at exactly the right time and place. The sound of that water hitting the fire at the right time gave him such a happy, joyful feeling inside.

Sammy used his new ability again and again until the fire was completely out.

His face lit up as he heard everybody clapping and cheering.

"Hurray, Sammy! You did it!" all the animals exclaimed.

Sammy felt very special for the first time in a very long time. He knew he now had a *special ability — being able to hold onto the water for a long time and knowing exactly when and where to let it all go.*

As the days went by, Sammy was *able to discover other abilities* that he had forgotten about. He thought to himself, "Once you know how to hold onto the water, you can hold onto anything successfully."

Just at that moment, Mr. Camel came walking by.

Sammy saw him and shouted, "Watch this, Mr. Camel!" He went over to the tent and picked up a heavy wooden beam. He brought the beam all the way over to the center of the tent where it belonged. As he gently let it down, Sammy felt wonderful inside.

Imagine seeing him letting go of the beam so securely and hearing it land so gently.

Mr. Camel smiled at Sammy and said, *"You have learned that and much, much more.* As you continue to be an important part of this circus, *you will continue to learn more and more each day."*

Weeks later, after the tent was up, Sammy was practicing balancing on a box so he could join the elephant act when he got bigger. He saw Mr. Camel again.

Mr. Camel reminded Sammy, *"Anytime you want to see yourself doing anything in the future, just remember all the important things you've already learned. You can learn anything else you need, just by taking your time and holding on to those happy memories."*

Sammy nodded his head. "Thank you, Mr. Camel," he said, "for reminding me of something I knew all along."